unilla Wolde

TOMMY
builds a house

strations copyright © 1969 unilla Wolde

right © 1971 Brockhampton Press Ltd

in Great Britain

OUGHTON MIFFLIN COMPANY BOSTON

10,484

Tommy is getting ready to build a house. So he puts on his carpenter's overalls.

Then he looks to see if he has all the tools he needs. There are a hammer and a saw, pliers, a drill, and two screwdrivers, which he puts in his useful pocket. There are also lots of nails and screws.

Tommy puts some tools back in his toolbox and asks Mother if she would like to help. But Mother is very busy adding up how much things cost and says, "Not just now, dear."

Father is busy too, reading all the news in the newspaper. But he promises to help Tommy if he needs it.

Bear seems to be the only one who isn't busy doing something. Bear would like to help Tommy build his house.

So they begin right away.
Tommy starts by sawing a long plank of wood.
It is very hard work.

The saw wobbles all over the place.
But Tommy keeps trying.

Finally Tommy gets the saw to work.

Bang, bang, bang, bang, bang.
Tommy makes a lot of noise
hammering and nailing pieces of
wood together.
He has to be careful not to hit
his fingers.

And some of the nails do not
go in straight.

Tommy's house begins to take shape.
It has walls and a roof.

Tommy uses his pliers to take out all the crooked nails.

"Boy," says Tommy. "This is going to be a great house."

Bear thinks it is too dark inside.
So Tommy makes a lot of little windows with his drill.

He puts in some screws to hold the
boards together better.

Then Tommy gets inside and peeks through one of the windows. "I can see the whole world," he says.

The little wooden house is finished.

Tommy cleans up the sawdust, and puts
away his tools.

And Tommy and Bear move in.

"Let's have a party," says Tommy.

They invite Mother. She has finished
adding up costs now and says, "Thank you
very much."

Then Tommy asks Father if he would like to come to a party. "Certainly," says Father, folding up his newspaper.

They all get inside the little wooden house.
"It's a bit crowded," says Father, laughing.
"But a nice kind of crowded," says Tommy.